PUFFIN BOOKS

RHYMES FOR THE TIMES

Born in Kasauli (Himachal Pradesh) in 1934, Ruskin Bond grew up in Jamnagar (Gujarat), Dehradun, New Delhi and Simla. His first novel, *The Room on the Roof*, which was written when he was seventeen, received the John Llewellyn Rhys Memorial Prize in 1957. Since then, he has written over 500 short stories, essays, novellas (including *The Adventures of Rusty* and *The Room of Many Colours*) and more than seventy books for children.

He received the Sahitya Akademi Award for English writing in India in 1992, the Padma Shri in 1999 and the Padma Bhushan in 2014. He lives in Landour, Mussoorie, with his extended family.

Ruskin Bond

PUFFIN BOOKS

Puffin Books is an imprint of the Penguin Random House group of companies
whose addresses can be found at global.penguinrandomhouse.com

Published by Penguin Random House India Pvt. Ltd
4th Floor, Capital Tower 1, MG Road,
Gurugram 122 002, Haryana, India

Penguin Random House India

First published in Puffin Books by Penguin Random House India 2024

10 9 8 7 6 5 4 3 2 1

ISBN 9780143459835

Book design and layout by Samar Bansal
Typeset in IM Fell Double Pica
Printed at Replika Press Pvt. Ltd, India

www.penguin.co.in

FSC www.fsc.org MIX Paper | Supporting responsible forestry FSC™ C016779

Rhymes for the Times

A Book *of* Poems, Limericks
and Nonsense Verse

RUSKIN BOND

PUFFIN BOOKS
An imprint of Penguin Random House

Author's Note

It seems a long time ago since we were all confined to our homes because of COVID-19. It was particularly frustrating for young people who wanted to get on with their lives.

And for old people, such as myself, it was a period of waiting. Would we survive or would we get it, too?

To make matters worse, I had a skin infection which kept me awake at night. For weeks, months, I couldn't sleep. It was as though hundreds of ants were crawling over me. There was some relief during the day, but the itching and irritation would start off as soon as I went to bed.

And so, in order to get through the night, I started writing nonsense verse—limericks, nonsensical couplets, silly poems, sometimes something serious or contemplative. But it was mostly nonsense, like that strange café that served crow's feet and other delicacies. And it helped me stay sane.

As dawn broke and the imaginary ants went home, I would fall asleep, exhausted but in a way creatively satisfied.

My notebooks were full of nonsense. Some of it I have thrown away. Some of it I have kept for your amusement, dear reader. And because it shows you that words, too, can have a healing touch.

Read a little, write a little, pray a little, laugh a little and sing a little!

Ruskin Bond
Landour, 2024

Mimi

Mimi is our cat
She sleeps all day.
But at night, she's a hunter
She's up and away
Into cupboards and corners
All over the house
She's out to confront
A terrified mouse!
Mimi's no kitten.
She's seven this year.
But when she's out hunting
Those mice disappear.

The Love of Two Bears

There was a handsome young polar bear
Who wanted a partner in his life to share.
When he met a sweet bruin upon the ice
He gave her fish, and she thought he was nice.
And they made such a happy and handsome pair
As they hunted together just everywhere.
Oh, for the life of a polar bear!

Look Inwards, Traveller

We reach for the stars.
In space, we go travelling.
While deep in the earth's bowels
Great fires are burning.
Who will escape, then?
Not you and I, friend,
It's only first class
From here to the world's end.

Gone

Where are all the singing birds now?
Where have all the swallows gone?
Gone to their secret groves,
Where no man ever goes . . .

Aunt Elfie

Poor aunt Elfie
Lies cold and stiff,
She took a selfie
At the edge of a cliff.

River of Life

Mountain water is always best
Where it springs from its mother's verdant breast.
A fern-covered fissure in the rock's fine seam,
A trickle that ends in a mountain stream.
And the stream flows down to a bigger river.
Big river, swift river, running forever,
Never astop till it finds its home
In the ocean's all-embracing foam.
The mountain water flows down to the sea,
River of life for you and me.

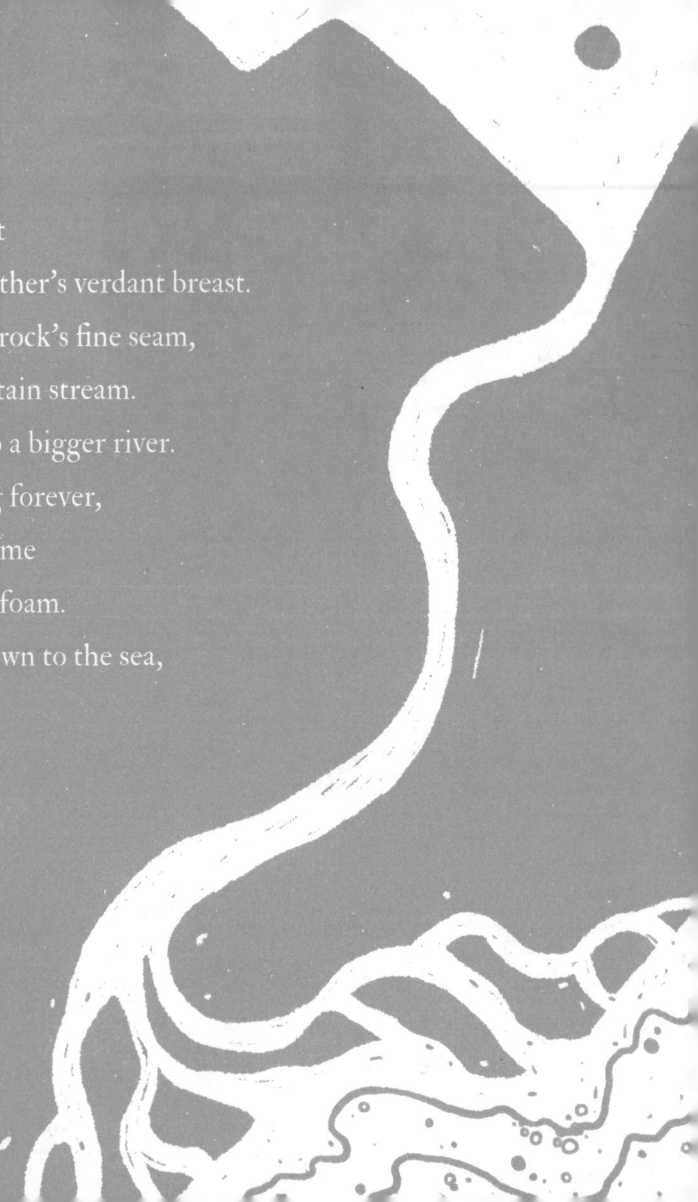

Under the Stairs

There's someone or something
Living under the stairs.
But whenever I look,
There's nobody there.
Sometimes, there's a whisper
And a sigh in the air.
But whenever I look,
There's nobody there.

* * *

Last night, when I came,
A shadow crept out;
A shadow from under the stairs.
It climbed up the wall
And went out on the roof,
A horrible thing with a cloven hoof.
Was there for a moment, right up there,
And then it was gone, the shadow and all,
And now there is nobody under the stairs.

The Man Who Laughed Too Much

There was a young man who laughed so much
That his head fell off in a cloud of dust.
'Don't worry, my dear,' said his loving mother.
'You'll soon have it back, as good as any other!'
She picked up his head and stitched it back on
'Do you feel it's a good fit?' she asked her son.
'It fits even better,' he said and laughed again.
His loving mother rescued it and said, 'I'll make it look new.'
And she stuck it back on with a pot of glue!
'Does it hurt very much?' she asked her fond son.
'Yes, it does a bit when I laugh or run.'
So, he learnt to laugh from deep within
And his tummy would make the most awful din.
When it rumbled and grumbled as he lay in his bed
Doing his best to save his fat head.

More About Mimi

Mimi is our cat,
And she's an aristocrat.
Her forebears hung out
With pharaohs in Egypt
And princes in Persia,
In fact, she's the cat's whiskers!
And I'm just an ordinary chap.
But I'm permitted
To brush her coat
And comb her silken fur.
And graciously she thanks me
With a soft and gentle purr.

A Cricket Sings

When I was feeling lonely
With the fading of the light,
I heard a cricket singing
In the stillness of the night.
Just a lonesome cricket singing
For the coming of the day,
But for me it brought glad tidings
As it swept my blues away.

The Grammar of Food

Sometimes, I feel like 'English' fare:
Sausages and mash
(With mustard just a dash),
A shepherd's pie,
A cutlet—or even two.
My words sound appetizing
When I'm eating Irish stew.

Catty Words

The cat has lent its name to a number of English words and expressions. For instance:

Catnap: A brief period of sleep during a busy day

Catwalk: A very narrow pathway in a restricted space

Cat burglar: A thief who gets into a house via the roof or upper floor

Cat mint: A mint-flavoured plant to which cats are partial

Caterwauling: Screaming and screeching like cats, usually at night

The cat's whiskers: Looking very special, all dressed up (sometimes used derisively, too)

A catty person (slang): A gossipy, malicious talker

Cat-o'-nine tails: A whip, used on sailors in the eighteenth century

Corvus Splendens

Oh, splendid crow! Now there's a name
to take you down the halls of fame.
A common crow. And yet so sleek
His plumage dims the eagle's beak.
And if you leave an open door
He'll sidle up across the floor.
And with one swoop, your egg is gone—
Your breakfast done, his just begun!
Don't leave your breakfast on display
This wily bird will take away
Your egg, your toast, your precious ham,
And leave you with a bit of jam.

The Hippo Who Wanted to Dance

A hippo who wanted to dance
Got a job with the Ballet de France.
Where he pranced on his toes,
And stood on his nose,
Till the audience fell into a trance.

So our Hippo then started a school,
For those who would dance by the rule.
But some did the Tango.
And some the Fandango,
And some just danced to be cool.

Do You Believe in Ghosts?

'Do you believe in ghosts?'
Asked the passenger
On platform number three.
'I'm a rational man,' said I,
'I believe in what I can see—
Your hands, your feet, your beard.'
'Then, look again,' said he,
And promptly disappeared!

Don't Give Up on God

Don't give up on God.
Some prayers are answered
Some are not.
But just to know that someone's there
Can mean a lot.

Do It Right

If you feel like singing,
Sing.
If you feel like painting,
Paint.
If you feel like writing,
Write.
Whatever you do,
Whether running a race
or travelling in space,
Do it right.
Do it right!

Choosing A Pet

I'd like to keep a pet,

but

Dogs bite

Cats scratch

Donkey bray

And rabbits poop all day.

Goats can be fun,

But they nibble away

At anything green

That they find on the way—

Granny's prized sweet peas

And Grandpa's French beans

All go the way

Of grasses and greens.

Grandpa kept a fox
A handsome young male,
Sadly, it meant
That his chicken farm failed.

But Granny kept a hen,
Her name was Henrietta.
She was a person of character,
No fox came near her.

When she was angry,
She flew at me
And kicked my spectacles off!

I'd like to keep a camel.
They have character, too.
And those beautiful necks
And humps and bumps . . .
Yes, a camel will do!
But where do I keep him?
This isn't a zoo.

But the world is a zoo
And there's a zookeeper, too.
Hundreds and thousands
Of creatures great and small,
He watches over all.

Camels and tortoises
Zebras and porpoises.
Bullfrogs and buffaloes
Giraffe and flamingoes.
Tigers, ants, snails
Polar bears and mountain quails!
And funny humans too
All go to make this world
A wonderful, crazy zoo!

Another Man Who Laughed His Head Off

There was a young man who laughed so
Much that his head fell off in a cloud of dust.
So they stuck it back on with a pot of glue,
And soon, his head looked as good as new.
But that silly young man, he laughed again,
And this time, his head fell in the drain.
But they stitched it back on with a needle and twine
Till his head looked swell and perfectly fine.
But he laughed too loud and he laughed some more
Till man and his head both fell to the floor.
So they got them together, securely bound
With his fat head facing the wrong way round.

Red

Bright red, the poinsettia glows
And rhododendrons in the snow.
Red poppies dancing in the breeze
And bulbuls in the coral trees.
Then at dawn a crimson flood,
Bright red; the colour of blood.
Tomatoes shining in the sun
And apples ripening one by one.
Bright red the flame tree in the spring,
And on cold days, the redstarts sing.
Red is the rose and the heather bud,
And the world is a fountain filled with blood.

The Characteristics of Some of Our Birds

The splendour of the peacock.
The cheekiness of sparrows.
The homeliness of pigeons.
The perseverance of the woodpecker.
The craftiness of the crow.
The merriment of the mynas.
The gossiping of babblers.
The solitude of the owl.
The devotion of the sarus crane.
The greed of the seagulls.
The omniscience of the eagle.
The complaint of the barbet.
The optimism of the penguins.
The parroting of the parrots.
The broken melody of the whistling thrush.

Another Day at the Strange Café

'Waiter! What's this in my soup?
It looks like a caterpillar.'
'Quite right, sir. It's quite expensive.
But very delicious! It came all the way from Mauritius.'
'Crawled here, I suppose. Or did it come as a chrysalis?
And what are these little bugs swimming around in my soup?'
'Oh those, sir, they're burrowing beetles from Brazil.
Very nutritious.'
'And this jelly in the middle? I suppose it's edible?'
'The jelly's incredible, sir. It's taken from the stomach
Of an alligator. This one had just eaten the ship's navigator.
But if you feel queasy, sir, you can wash it all down
With a bottle of Jumna water. It's full of minerals.
Or might you prefer some wine?'
'Elder wine, I see. I expect from the older people.'
'Over sixties, sir. It was felt they were living too long.'
'Well, I'm glad I'm fifty-nine!'

'Oh, you'd make a very fine wine, sir.
That florid complexion would be just the right hue.
And you look as though you have been in the cellars for a hundred years—or more!
Is there anything else I can bring you, sir?'
'No, take it all away. But on second thought,
You can leave the caterpillar.
It looks quite appetizing.'

Limericks and More

There was an old witch who would glide,
On her broom through the sky far and wide.
She had a black cat,
And a funny old bat,
And she'd take them along for the ride.

***

There was a young man from Calcutta,
Who spread on his toast lots of butter.
Then he added plum jam
(or in preference, some ham),
That chubby young man from Calcutta.

***

There was a girl called Lisa,
Who was constantly dining on pizza.
When she grew stout and long
She picked up a prong
And straightened the tower of Pisa!

***

On Shimla's slopes, on Jakko Hill,
A phantom lady haunts us still.
She carries her head beneath her arm,
But don't be scared, she means no harm.
She's the resident ghost of Shimla town,
And she haunts the hill from dusk to dawn.

***

A turkey said gobble-gobble
Its wattle went wabble-wabble,
And we merrily dined
On roast turkey and wine,
And wobbled home, hobble-hobble.

Failed Vampire

There was an old vampire called Bud
Who tired of a diet of blood.
So he tried turkey roast,
And caviar on toast,
And resigned from Count Dracula's club.

Earth Song

Seeds fall
Spade spreads
Water falls
Earth drinks.
Roots grasp
Leaves sprout
Buds flower
Petals fall.
Fruits ripen
Trees grow tall
Monsoon comes.

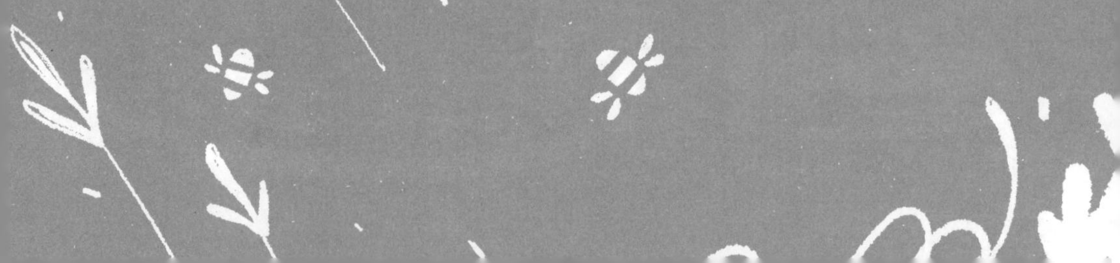

Rivers flood
Buffaloes wade
Fertile mud
September's here.
Gentle sun
Earthworms turn
Soft winds blow
The seeds we sow
Take root again.
Birds and bees
Sing their refrain
The days grow long,
The earth spins on.

Nobody Knows

Where did the virus come from?
From bats or dogs
Or cats and frogs
Or stinking bogs
Or rotting logs
Where did the virus come from?

When will it come, and when will it go
Swift as a river in the monsoon flow.
It travels wherever it cares to roam,
And only the children are left alone.

Does it fear children?
Nobody knows.
Nobody knows where it comes and goes.

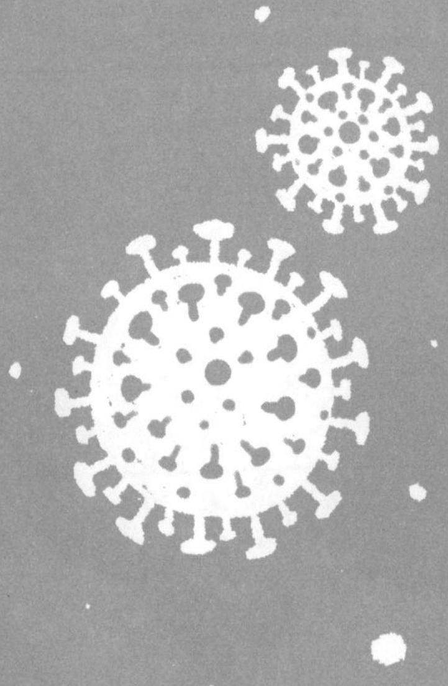

Four Pretty Girls

Four pretty girls
Sitting on a wall,
One was short
And one was tall.
One was slim
But not too thin,
And one had dimples
In her chin.
Four pretty girls
So bright and neat,
The sun came down
And touched their feet.

A Time to Feast

Oh! What fun it is to be
A parrot in a mango tree,
A rabbit in a cabbage patch,
A heron on a buffalo's back,
A bee upon a honeysuckle,
A polar bear with lots of fish,
An ant in Granny's sugar dish!
A squirrel feasting on a nut,
A snail upon a rose in bud,
An earthworm in a patch of mud.

A cow upon a grassy knoll,
A sunbird on a tender vine,
A mouse with lots of cheese to eat,
A cat with cream upon its cheek,
A donkey with a carrot to munch,
A seagull with a crab for lunch.

Here's Granny with a cake to bake
A cake with icing and a plum.
So, happy birthday, little one!
Have fun, grow strong and tall,
With all good creatures great and small.

Two Lovely Ducks

Our hero took aim with his bat.
Heard the dreaded cry, 'How's that?'
Caught behind wicket
Playing T20 cricket
He blamed his bad shot on the wicket.

Another day, another game
Our hero walked out once again
Determined to improve his game
But lo! Before he'd made a score
He was given out, leg before
And another duck beside his name.

A Spinner from Hooghly

There was a young bowler from Hooghly
Who bowled an amazing googly,
Whether clean bowled or caught
You'd be out for a naught,
To that clever young bowler from Hooghly!

Legend

The great gardener roamed in his domain,
And gave each brilliant flower a name.
But there was one, concealed within a shady nook.
'Please name me too!' the soft petals shook.
The gardener paused, came to a stop,
He smiled, 'Your name's forget-me-not.'

The Money-Go-Round

’Tis money that makes the world go round,
The mighty dollar, the fretful pound,
The yen, the yuan, the modest cent,
Some sums are borrowed, some are lent.
Some buy stocks and some buy shares
With raging ‘bulls’, unhappy ‘bears’.
Yes, money makes the world go round
Though some folks keep theirs underground.
The world grows grim; the future is dim
Take care, my friend, put something by.
Yes, money talks
And it’s saying goodbye.

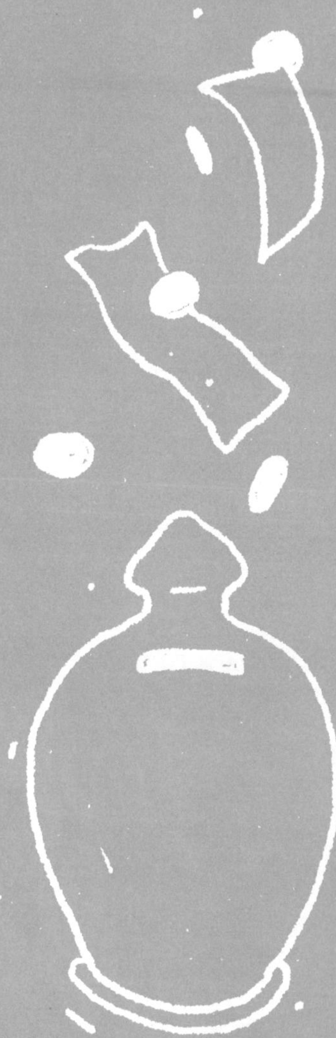

Quiet Places

Quiet places
There aren't many.
An old library
A forgotten tomb
A long-deserted room
A forest when the wind is still
A shelter on a lonely hill
A school where all the kids have gone
A battlefield when the war is done.

Cheer Up

'Tis a sad world.
Full of sighing, crying,
Whining, fighting, dying.
Cheer up, my friends,
There's always a book for company.
Jeeves, or Monsieur Poirot,
Or Henry D. Thoreau,
Or even Henry Miller,
And a glass of sherry,
With your dinner.

Down it Goes

Whatever I eat
Becomes me.
Strawberry jam,
Pickles or ham,
Sausages, mash,
And mustard a dash.
Curry and rice
With plenty of spice
Cucumber, tomatoes
And French-fried potatoes.
Sardines on toast
And gravy with roast
Pizza and pastries at tea
Whatever I eat
Becomes me.

Lone Fox Dancing

As I walked home last night
I saw a lone fox dancing
In the cold moonlight.
I stood and watched.
Then took the low road,
Knowing the night was his by right.
Sometimes, when words ring true,
I'm like a lone fox dancing
In the morning dew.

Crown Jewels

Rubies from Burma
And diamonds from Ind,
For these and much more
Great men had sinned.
Gold from Africa
Sapphires from Ceylon,
All these now glow
In a monarch's crown.

The Boy from Chennai

There was a bright boy from Chennai,
Whose skill at playing chess was so high,
That he won every game,
From Mongolia to Spain,
And brought his fame home to Chennai.

The Prince from Rangoon

There was a young prince from Rangoon
Who married the Princess Half-moon.
He discovered too late
That she turned into a snake
Every night, by the light of the moon.

Just for Fun

Along came a man with a gun
Who shot a big snake, just for fun.
But then came another
(The python's big brother)
And swallowed that man, just for fun.

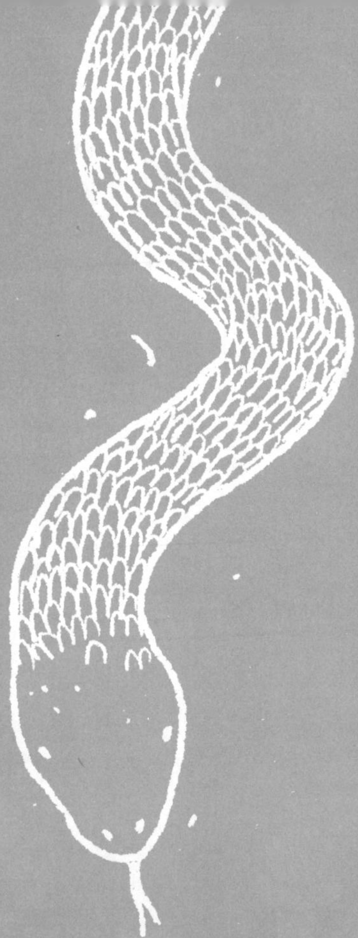

Sleigh Ride

A young man went riding his sleigh
In a reckless and hazardous way.
Faster he went and pacier,
Till he shot off the edge of a glacier
And he hasn't been seen to this day.

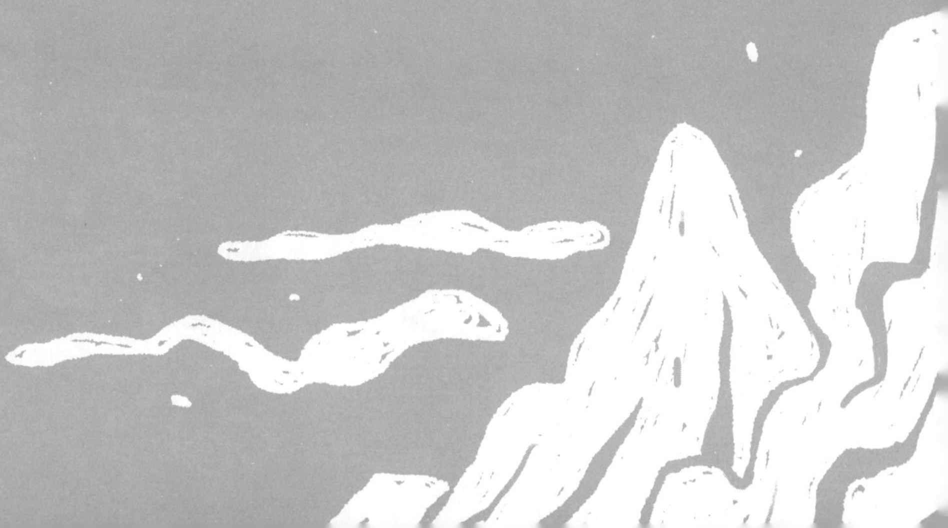

Revisiting the Strange Café

'Waiter! There's a fish in my soup!'
'Exactly, sir, with the compliments of the chef.'
'But it's alive! It's swimming around; what am I to do with it?'
'Quite simple, sir. All you have to do is catch
It by the tail, I mean fin . . . fish it out of the
Soup bowl, open your mouth, and drop it on your
tongue. The little fish will do the rest. It will
swim down your gullet with the soup, and settle
down in your tummy. Voila! Loop the loop!'

Make Room for Elephants

Make room for elephants; their precious space
Is being taken away by the human race.
Their strength is matched by a sense of fun.
Theirs is the right to a place in the sun.
For thousands of years, they've roamed this place,
And they walk the earth with amazing grace.
Make room for elephants,
Give them their space!

Falling in Love Again

Gosh! But it's plain,
I'm falling in love again.
Just one kiss
And I'm dished.
Saturated
Infatuated
Completely deflated
I'm done for!
I've never before
Been struck to the core.

By someone so . . . so . . .
Different . . .
Reticent . . .
Cognizant . . .
Of my complete surrender.
I'll be good, I'll be tender
Just live with me forever
In the land of Never-Never.
Help! But it's plain,
I'm falling in love again.

Dinner at the Strange Café

'Waiter! What's for dinner?'

'Good evening, sir. Dinner's very special today. Breast of crow with bread and sauce. And if you care for something sweet, there's snail syrup or, if you prefer, moths preserved in strawberry jam.'

'And have you anything to drink?'

'There's toadstool wine, sir. Or would you care for sherry?'

'What's in the sherry?'

'Bee venom, sir. It gives it that extra punch!'

'Fine, I'll have the sherry.'

'Very good, sir. You are our most valuable customer. The owner would like to pay his respects. Here is he, sir. Please meet Dr Rattlesnake.'

The owner spread his mouth, revealing a forked tongue and purple teeth.

'Welcome to our modest establishment,' he said. 'It's always a pleasure to serve you. And one day, we must have you on our menu. Buttered Bond with baked potatoes. How does that sound?'

'Not so good,' said I.

'Tandoori Ruskin, then,' he hissed. 'Think it over, sir. You won't be missed!'

Nonsensical Grammar

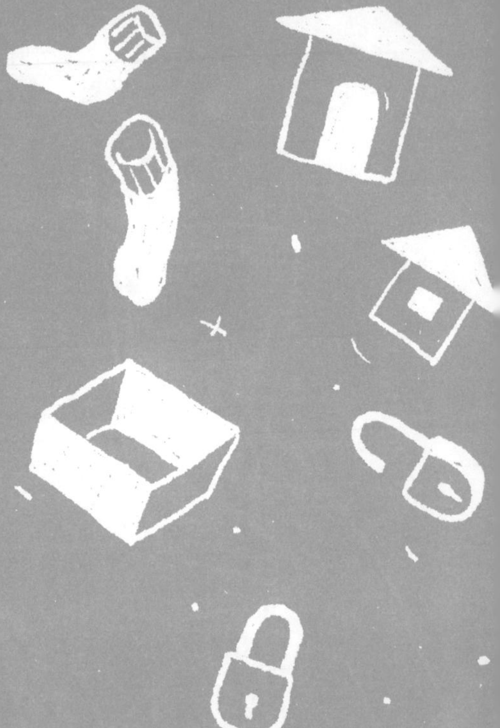

If two of a mouse are called mice,
Why aren't two of a house called 'hice'?
If two of a man are called men,
Why aren't two of a fan called 'fen'?
And if two of a foot are called feet,
Why aren't two of a boot called 'beet'?

* * *

If fox is spelt fox
Why can't socks be spelt 'sox'?
And if box is spelt box
Why can't locks be spelt 'lox'?
If fix is spelt fix
Why can't tricks be spelt 'trix'?

* * *

If I stare at the stair,
I see a bear running bare.
In search of my horse,
I call till I'm hoarse.
And I hear that it's here
But oh dear! It's not a horse . . . it's a deer!

The Idiot's Alphabet

Here are some of the things (animal or vegetable) that I was called by one of my teachers when I was a reluctant schoolboy:

A: You're an Ass, Bond! (I'd heard that before.)

B: You're a Bird-brain. (Thank you, kind sir.)

C: You're going Cuckoo! (Crazy, he means.)

D: A Donkey! A disgrace to this place. (Can it get worse?)

E: You sit there looking like an Eggplant. (Also known as a brinjal or aubergine)

F: 'The Fool of the class.' (A title I cherish!)

G: You've got the mind of a Goat, Bond. (I thought I was a donkey, sir.)

H: All you can do is eat like a Horse! (Sir, I thought I was a goat.)

I: You're as slow as an Inchworm. Get on with it, you idiot! (I'm inching along, sir.)

J: Bond, you're a Jackass! (Thank you for the promotion, sir.)

K: Go back to Kindergarten. (If you'll come with me, sir.)

L: Only a Lunatic would want you in his class. (I'm glad you really want me, sir.)

M: You're the Monkey of the class, Bond. (Thank you for making me a monster, sir.)

N: You're a Nincompoop! (An old-fashioned endearment. Look it up.)

O: You look Owlish, Bond. (I do have that kind of face.)

P: The Perfect Pupil. (Said with sarcasm!)

Q: Have you no Questions, Bond? (Yes, sir. How are you keeping, sir?)

R: A Rapscallion! You don't belong here. (Where shall I go, sir?)

S: How Stupid can you get? (As stupid as you want me to be, sir.)

T: As slow as a Tortoise. (The one who won the race?)

U: Bond, you're an 'Ullu'! (In Hindi or Urdu, sir?)

V: You're the VIP of the class. Always last! (Recognition, at last.)

W: You're a Write-off, bond. You can't even write. (But I can spell, sir.)

X: The mark usually placed after my sums.

Y: You're a Yokel. Go back to your village. (I'm in it, sir.)

Z: Zero! Another zero for you, Bond. Are you listening?

Zzzz . . . Bond has fallen asleep.

Obit for a Climber

On Everest's slope
He took his stance
Then perished
In an avalanche.

A Small Helping

I thank you, Lord,
For this small fish,
'Tis better than
An empty dish.

Where Have They Gone?

When car horns blare
And bells keep ringing,
I have to ask:
Are birds still singing?

Mouth-Watering Menus

Mouth-watering menus
Tempt the wise,
But light suppers
Make long lives.

Let's Touch

Covid's gone,
It's on the wane,
Let's touch each other
Once again.

Five Sleepers

Don't wake any of the following:

Tigers

Snakes

Babies

Strange dogs

Bees

Can you think of anyone else we should be careful not to wake?

Your big brother, perhaps.

Lines Written at 2 A.M.

Oh, life is just a riddle.
A silly sort of fiddle,
A doodle-dandy diddle,
A time to laugh or cry.

It's really just a muddle.
A fiddle-faddle huddle,
A paddle in a puddle,
A time to laugh or cry.

Sometimes, it's all a puzzle.
A kind of a jigsaw juggle,
A dream or just a bubble,
A life of toil and trouble,
A time to laugh or cry.

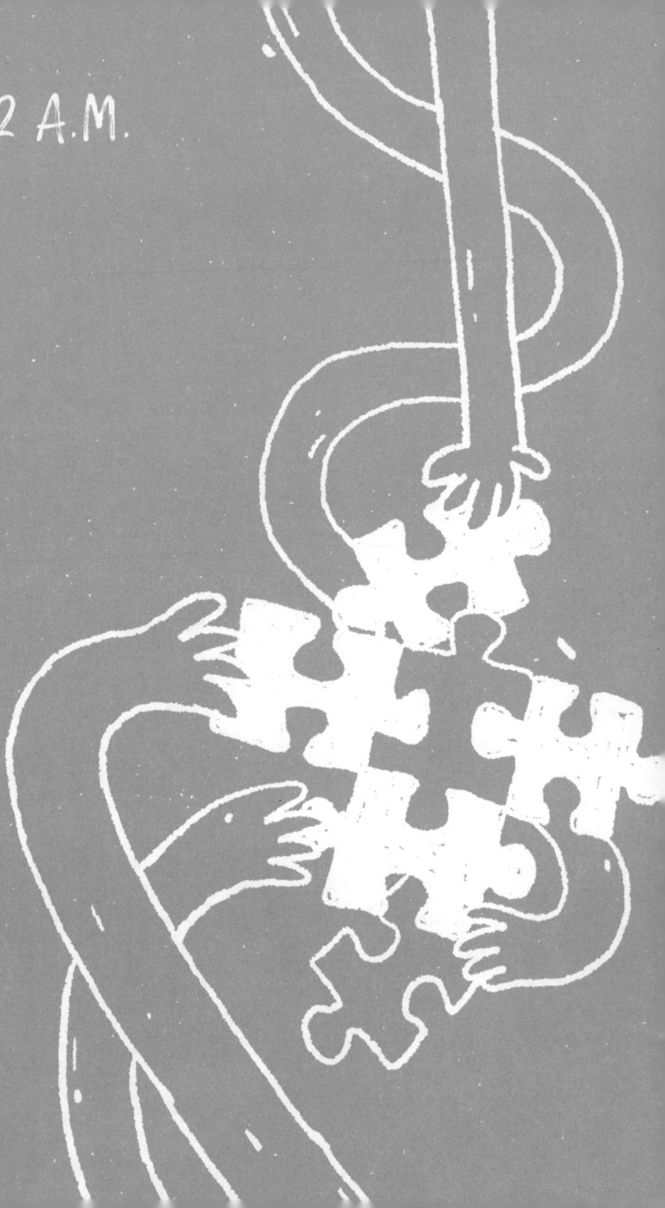

We're All the Same

Great men must burp,
And saints must sneeze,
And kings grow wobbly in the knees,
And so, when people laugh at you,
Remember—they're just as funny in the loo.

Amazing Grace

Men kill from greed,
And sometimes for pleasure,
Hunters they have been since time beyond measure,
Tigers and lions will kill for their dinner.
And likewise the anteater, his tongue all aquiver.
Big fish eat small fish; it's a whale of a feast,
And swim for your life if a shark's near your feet!
'Tis the way of the ocean, the law of the sea,
The law of big brother who's looking for me.

A snake strikes dead,
A python will swallow you whole—
And keep some for tomorrow—
But you won't find the elephant
Killing for meat.

He'll dine on this bamboo,
And the grass at his feet.
The fruits of the earth are his to command,
And he'll trumpet his thanks all over the land.

Their trunks are their trumpets,
Their feet are the pillars
That hold up the sky
And its cloud messengers.
And at night, when they dance
In their secretive place,
The gods look down—
Amazed at such grace.

Count the Days

Cocks crowing
Crows cawing
Cattle crawling
Cowherds calling
Cream curdling
Crickets chirping
Children counting
Crackers crackling
Church bells chiming
Cooks conniving
Christmas coming!

More Limericks

There was a young lady in Kutch
Who lived with a sweet *muggermachh*.
She fed it rice,
And hundreds of mice,
Till it cried, 'Oh, I love you so much!'

***

There was a young girl in Bangalore.
Who gobbled up cake and wanted more,
When her tummy soon burst
(as distended, it must),
Her buttons rained down on Mangalore!
(With apologies to the good people of Bangalore.)

***

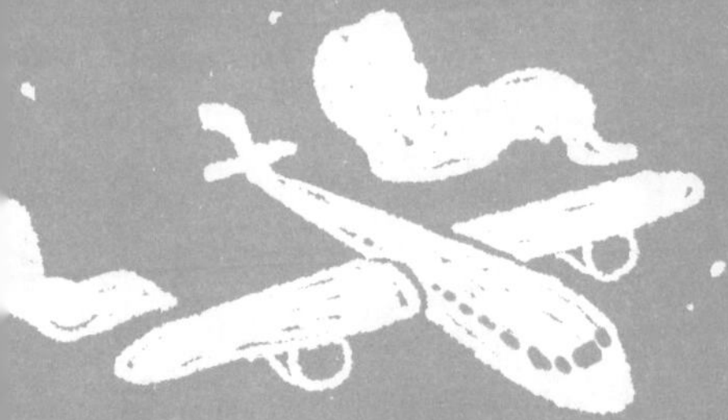

There was a young man in Mumbai
Who wanted to fly to Shanghai.
But he took the wrong flight
In the dead of the night
And the plane set him down in Dubai.

* * *

There was a most handsome young actor
(God's gift, we are told by Max Factor),
But he proved to be lax
In paying income tax,
And ended up driving a tractor.

* * *

There was a young man who could swim
From Sri Lanka to Cape Comorin.
He had a long nose
And prehensile toes
And a tailbone that looked like a fin.

And More . . .

The ghost of a writer called Kipling,
Walked up to where we were tippling,
'Excuse me, bartender,
But do you serve spirits?'
And vanished away in a twinkling!

If Mice Could Roar

If mice could roar
And elephants soar,
And trees grow up in the sky;
If tigers could dine
On biscuits and wine,
And the fattest of men could fly!
If pebbles could sing
and bells didn't ring,
And preachers were lost in the post;
If a tortoise could run
And losses be won,
And bullies be buttered on toast;
If a song brought a shower
And a gun grew a flower,
This world would be nicer than most!

Granny's Kitchen Proverbs

Better a small fish than an empty dish.

* * *

There is skill in all things, even in making porridge.

* * *

Light suppers make for long lives.

* * *

Don't let your tongue cut your own throat.

* * *

Bears love honey, and what's good for bears is good for boys.

* * *

Even a snail will cross a busy road to reach a lettuce leaf.

* * *

Granny to young Ruskin:

'No chocolate pudding until you have eaten your vegetables.'

* * *

And Manu the law-giver said: 'Respect your food.'

Think about it.

A little food will help you think.

Too much, and you will surely sink.

* * *

Too many cooks spoil the broth.

* * *

Granny: 'The crust of the loaf is the best part.'

Waste not, want not.

* * *

Song of the Brave New World

(to the tune of 'Where Have All the Flowers Gone')

Where has all our garbage gone?
To your green field, my son.
And where has all the plastic gone?
To our great seas, my son.
So, where has all our sewage gone?
Into our great rivers, son.
We've done our best for you, dear one,
The road to hell is almost done.

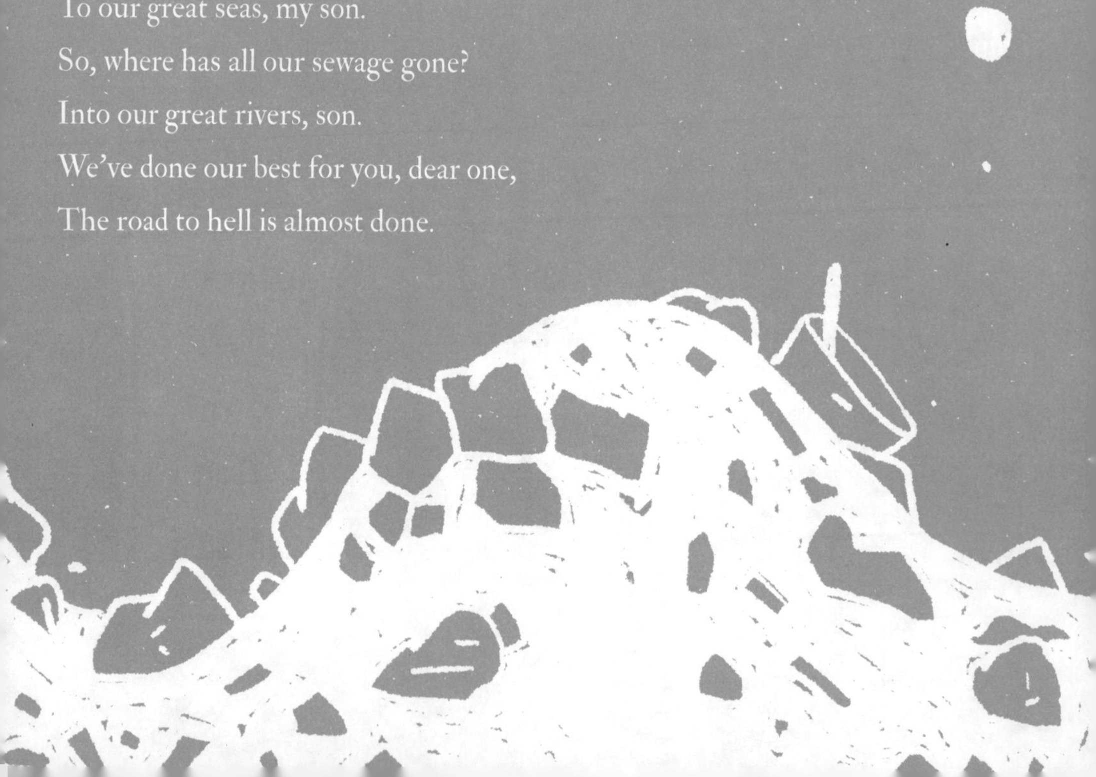

Self-Portrait

There was an old man in Landour
Who wanted young folk to laugh more.
So he wrote them a book,
And with laughter, they shook
As they rolled down the hill to Rajpore.

Afterword

In February of 1877, the tiny Himalayan hill station of Landour, at 7,500 feet, was cold. But that did not prevent Edward Lear from setting up his easel and painting a series of views of the great snow range to the north. He was a professional landscape artist, and his paintings can be seen today in the art galleries of London and Europe.

However, Edward Lear is better known today as a writer of nonsense verse and the inventor of the Limerick, a humorous refrain set to a particular rhyming pattern.

Lear was a strange-looking man with an oversized head and a misshapen body, given to epileptic seizures. No one wanted to marry him, and he led a rather lonely existence, but he gave the world, children in particular, a legacy of humourous verse that has enlivened many a home and classroom.

It was only recently that I learnt about his brief sojourn in Landour. From here, he went on to paint the Ganga at Haridwar and Benaras, as well as other Indian landscapes. I don't know if he wrote any limericks or nonsense verse while he was here, but it's the sort of place that lends itself to a little eccentricity. That's why I'm a part of the place!

My own humble attempts at verse (and worse) were written during the COVID-19 crisis, when I had some difficulty sleeping. Now that I'm sleeping soundly again, I've stopped writing nonsense verse!

Anyway, I hope this little book has helped to enliven your day or night.

As Ben Jonson once said, 'A little nonsense now and then gives pleasure to the best of men.'

And women. And children. And cats. And dogs. And dinosaurs.

Ruskin Bond
Landour, 2024

Acknowledgements

My thanks to the Puffin team: Sohini Mitra, Simran Kaur, Prerna Chatterjee and Samar Bansal for encouraging my nonsense, and to Siddhi Vartak for joining in the fun with her lively illustrations.

As always, my gratitude to my loving family for seeing me through a long, hard winter.

And a big thank you to the many kind readers who sent me gifts on my ninetieth birthday—pens, notebooks, paintings, potted plants, pickles and lollipops!

It was the best of all my birthdays.